Brutus
the
Bear

Brutus the Bear

Dave and Pat Sargent

Illustrated by
Blaine Sapaugh

Ozark Publishing, Inc.
P.O. Box 228
Prairie Grove, AR 72753

F
Sar   Sargent, Dave
       Brutus the Bear, by Dave and Pat Sargent.
Illus. by Blaine Sapaugh.
       Ozark Publishing, Inc., 1996.
       44P. Illus. (Animal Pride Series)
       Summary: When an innocent, naive young
bear finds a trotline of fish and begins to eat, he is
interrupted by a rock-salt shotgun.
       1. Bears I. Sargent, Pat. II. Title. III. Series.

ISBN Casebound 1-56763-078-2
ISBN Paperback 1-56763-006-5

Ozark Publishing, Inc.
P.O. Box 228
Prairie Grove, AR 72753
Ph: 1-800-321-5671

Printed in the United States Of America

Inspired by

the time Amber, her two sisters, and their mother were having a picnic with us at the farm. Amber was eight years old at the time. Just as she took the first bite out of her chicken leg, a bear stepped out from behind a tree. Needless to say, the bear enjoyed his meal.

Dedicated to

my granddaughter,
Amber Nichole Sargent Kassel.

Foreword

Brutus, an innocent, naive young bear, finds a trotline of fish and a beehive full of honey, and he thinks as he begins to eat, "How thoughtful of someone to leave this delicious food for me." Brutus learned that Farmer John had a shotgun filled with rock salt. Of course, he found out too late.

Contents

Brutus
the
Bear

One

Brutus the Black Bear

Brutus and his mama had been eating fish, berries, and honey when they could find it all summer long. They were storing up fat for the hard winter that lay ahead.

They ate from daylight till dark every day. At night, they couldn't see, so they would take a little nap and rest so that they could start hunting for food again at first light.

One morning when Brutus woke up from his nap, Mama Bear was gone. Brutus said to himself, "Mama probably went to get a drink or something and will be right back."

Brutus was still waiting when lunchtime came. Mama Bear hadn't come home, and he didn't know what to think.

Brutus was two years old now and old enough to be on his own. That's why Mama Bear had left him. It was time for him to make his own way.

By mid-afternoon, Brutus was so thirsty that he just had to find water. He located a stream not far away, and after drinking his fill of water, he returned to the place where he and Mama Bear had spent the night.

Brutus kept hoping and kept thinking that his mama would come home. Finally, the sun was setting, and there was still no sign of Mama Bear.

Brutus thought to himself, "I'm scared. I've never been alone before. I don't know what I'm going to do without Mama."

That night, Brutus lay on his bed, curled up in a ball, and thought about what he was going to do if Mama Bear didn't come back at all.

The next morning when the dark sky started turning to a light gray, Brutus woke up. He sat up and looked around. There was still no Mama Bear.

He stretched and yawned and rubbed his eyes, and said, "I guess I'm on my own. I'll have to make my own way."

He had not eaten the day before, and now, he was really hungry. He headed out in search of food.

It was early fall, and it wouldn't be long till hard winter set in. Brutus knew that he would have to find a warm place to sleep till spring. Of course, today, he was more interested in finding food than in finding a place to spend the winter.

As he looked around for something to eat, he saw that there were no berries left. This made hunting for food much more of a job.

Brutus made his way to the creek where he tried catching some fish. He didn't have much luck at first, but by noon, he had eaten his fill.

He decided to explore some new territory, so he headed out through the woods. He had traveled for about two hours when he came to a big field. There were several cows in the field, but they didn't seem to pay any attention to Brutus. He wasn't just real sure about the cows. He had never seen a cow before. He decided to walk around the edge of the field and not take a chance by getting too close to them.

While Brutus was making his way around the field, he heard something buzzing. He stopped for a moment and thought, "I've heard that sound before. I know what it is. It's honeybees."

Brutus began looking all around for a bee tree, but he couldn't find a tree with a hole in it. He decided that he would try watching for bees. When he finally spotted them, he was surprised to see that they were flying in and out of a big, white box. The white box was the bees' hive, and the beehive belonged to Farmer John.

Well, Brutus didn't have any way of knowing that the beehive belonged to Farmer John. All he knew was that honey was his favorite food.

He headed straight for the beehive and pulled the top off. When he did, the sky turned black with bees! And they were all after Brutus! He said, "I'm not afraid of getting stung a few times because the honey will be worth it!" He began dipping out the honey with both front paws and putting it into his mouth.

The honeybees attacked Brutus over and over while he ate the honey. Their stingers could not penetrate his thick fur, but they were getting plenty of good licks in on his nose and around his eyes.

Well, Brutus kept on eating honey, till he realized that he had a big problem. His nose was swollen so big that he could hardly breathe, and his eyes were almost swollen shut.

He stumbled off into the woods and lay down. He rubbed his sore, swollen eyes and his sore, swollen nose. The stings sure did hurt, but he thought the honey was worth the pain. He went to sleep and dreamed about a stream flowing with honey.

Two

The Rock-Salt Shotgun

E arly the next morning when
Brutus woke up, the swell-
ing had gone down a little. He

thought, "Boy, that honey would sure taste good for breakfast, but maybe I'd better wait till my swollen nose and my swollen eyes get better before I try that beehive again."

He made his way to a pond in Farmer John's field and got a much-needed drink of water. He had remembered passing by the pond the day before. While he was getting a drink, he noticed the water sloshing nearby and went to investigate.

Brutus found three large catfish that Farmer John had caught on a trotline. Now, Brutus loved catfish! It was his favorite fish,

so he ate all three of them for breakfast.

After eating the fish, he played in the pond for a while, then moseyed on back to the woods. When he reached the edge of the woods, he heard something coming. Brutus didn't know what the noisy thing was, but it was a tractor. He walked farther into the woods, then stopped and listened. The tractor was coming closer.

Brutus was curious, so he went to the edge of the field and watched. The tractor stopped at the pond, and the man got off and checked the trotline, the same line that Brutus had robbed.

Farmer John pulled in the line and said, "Looks like I didn't catch any fish last night. Hey, wait! There are fish bones on three of the hooks. The fish have been eaten!"

Farmer John looked all around and noticed the tracks that Brutus had left. He scratched his head and said, "A dad-blamed little ole bear ate my fish! I'd better check my beehive. Bears love honey. He probably ate it, too."

And sure enough, when Farmer John saw the hive, he could see that the bear had been into it.

He put the top back on the

beehive and said, "If I see that pesky little bear, I'll fill him full of rock salt with my shotgun."

Farmer John knew that Brutus was young. He could tell by the size of his tracks; the tracks were small.

The rock salt that Farmer John was going to use in his shotgun wouldn't hurt Brutus; it would only sting and burn. But, after a couple of shots of rock salt, Brutus wouldn't bother Farmer John anymore.

The truth is, Brutus didn't know that he should not eat Farmer John's honey, and he didn't know that he should not eat

Farmer John's fish. He thought that when he found something to eat, it was all right to eat it.

Farmer John climbed onto his tractor and started in the direction of his house.

Brutus moseyed out across the field. He felt a chill in the air and noticed that the wind had shifted. It was coming from the

northwest now, and this meant that it was time to start looking for a nice warm place to spend the winter.

So Brutus started looking for such a place. He searched all afternoon, but he found no den or cave to sleep in.

It was beginning to snow, and he knew that it would be a cold night. As the sun set and darkness covered the sky, he lay down on a big pile of leaves, curled up in a ball, and went to sleep.

The next morning when Brutus woke up, everything was white with snow. He stood up and shook the snow from his furry coat, and said, "I must find a nice warm place to spend the winter, even if it takes all day."

Brutus started across Farmer John's field. When he came to Farmer John's barn, he saw that it was full of hay. He thought, "This looks like a good place to sleep."

He opened the barn door and walked inside. The barn was full of nice, soft, fluffy hay, and Brutus said, "Oh, boy! This is the best place ever. I'll make this my winter home."

He made himself a nice, soft bed, then lay down and covered himself with hay. He said, "This hay will keep me nice and warm."

Three

Brutus Learns a Lesson

E arly the next morning, Farmer John was on his way to the barn to do his chores and noticed bear tracks in the snow. He knew right away that they belonged to Brutus, because they looked like the tracks he had found by his pond. Farmer John followed the tracks, and they led him straight to the barn door. He stopped and stroked his chin and said, "That dad-blamed little ole pesky bear is in my hay barn. I'll fix him!"

Farmer John ran to the house and grabbed his shotgun and loaded it with rock salt! He hurried back to the barn, opened the door, and stormed in. He waved the gun in the air and yelled, "Where are you, you dad-blamed little bear?"

The yell woke Brutus. He crawled out of the hay to see what was going on. When he spotted Farmer John with the shotgun, he knew he was in trouble! He took off for the door just as fast as his little fat, short legs would carry him. He pushed open the barn door, rushed outside, and ran for the woods!

Well, Farmer John let ole Brutus run a good ways, then he raised the shotgun and let go with the rock salt!

When the gun went off, Brutus stopped. He stood on his back legs and let out a loud roar! The rock salt burned and stung! He knew that he had to get away quickly, or he would be shot again. He dropped to the ground and, on all four feet, headed for the safety of the woods.

Farmer John wasn't trying to hurt the young bear, he just wanted to scare him away. It worked, because Brutus said, "I'll never go back there again!" He ran deep into the forest before stopping.

Brutus kept rubbing his backside. It was still burning and stinging. He ran until he found a place to lie down and rest.

Well, it was two long days before the rock salt stopped burning. Brutus remembered that he had to find a new home, so he searched up and down the creek. He found no den or cave big enough to crawl into. He was beginning to get weary. He thought, "Since the weather has warmed up a mite, maybe I can put off hibernating for a while."

While Brutus was sitting down resting, he thought, "I'm

getting hungry. I need to find something good for breakfast."

He started searching for berries, then remembered that the berries were all gone. He stopped in his tracks and said, "Honey! That's what I could eat! I could go back to the edge of that farmer's field and get some honey out of that big, white box."

Brutus took off at a fast shuffle. He stopped when he got to the edge of the field and said, "Boy! I'm glad I thought of this. That honey will sure taste good. I love honey!"

When he started toward the beehive again, he stopped and said, "I wonder where that farmer with the shotgun is?" He looked all around, then he took off across the open field.

Brutus said, "I think I'll check the pond first. There might be a fish on that line. I'll save the honey for dessert."

As Brutus ran, he looked all around to see if the farmer was anywhere in sight. When he reached the pond, he went to the spot where he had found the trotline, but the trotline was gone.

He said, "I wonder where that trotline is? I remember finding three fish on a line, right here in this exact spot. Maybe the farmer moved it."

He quickly searched under every big rock, and checked every stick at the edge of the pond to see if he could find a line attached.

When Brutus had almost circled the pond, he saw a broken tree branch sticking in the ground. Tied to the branch was a dirty white cord that angled down into the water.

Brutus reached down and, with his big paw, took hold of the line and tugged. When he tugged on the line, the water in front of the line started churning, and he knew that he had found a fish. He began pulling in the line.

When the first fish neared the bank, it began flipping and flopping, splashing water all over Brutus. He wasted no time eating the fish, then he hauled in another one. And just as before, Brutus got three big catfish off Farmer John's trotline.

When he finished eating, he wiped his mouth with the back of his front paw. Then, he thought about the beehive. He said, with a grin on his face, "Now for dessert!"

Brutus glanced all around as he headed for the big, white box. When he reached the beehive, he ripped off the top and scooped up a paw full of honey.

He was using both front paws, shoveling honey into his mouth. He had forgotten all about keeping an eye out for the farmer.

Farmer John had been on guard for the last two days. He searched high and low for Brutus. His shotgun was loaded with rock salt. He was ready for that bear! And this time, he had brought along Barney the Bear Killer. He didn't want Barney to kill the little bear like he had killed that mean ole grizzly. Farmer John just wanted Barney to scare the little bear so he would leave his bee-hive alone.

As he walked past the pond, he saw at a glance that his trotline had been robbed again.

Now, Brutus was having so much fun eating honey that he had completely forgotten everything else. He was shoveling honey in as fast as he could! It was all over his paws, and all over his arms, and was dripping off his chin.

Suddenly, there was a bay from the hound dog, a shout, and a loud *Boom*, and Brutus felt the stinging rock salt hit his backside again!

Farmer John had seen Brutus raiding his beehive and had let go with both barrels! He yelled, "You dad-blamed little ole pesky bear! I'll teach you to stay away from my beehive! I'll teach you to stay away from my trotline, too!"

Brutus jumped up and down and rubbed his backside with his sticky paws. He turned around just in time to see Farmer John pull a sack from his pocket and thought, "Oh, no! I'd better get out of here fast! He's loading that shotgun again!"

He lit out for the woods at a gallop on all four feet, like a horse. When Brutus was only three steps from the woods and safety, he heard the shotgun boom again.

He felt the rock salt hit him in the backside, then he heard Farmer John yell, "I gotcha that time, you pesky little varmint! Now, stay away from my beehive, and stay out of my fishing pond! You can get your fish out of the river!"

Brutus learned a valuable lesson that day. He made his home on Farmer John's place, but he had learned to respect the property of others.

He wandered onto a part of the farm that he didn't even know existed, for he had never been that far away from home before. He finally located a nice-sized cave in the side of a bluff, down by the

Illinois River. The river was full of fish, and he saw dozens and dozens of berry bushes. He knew that he would always have enough to eat.

Farmer John's farm was big. It covered many square acres. Brutus was very happy and contented. He had plenty to eat, and he had the run of the woods.

When Brutus grew up, he was a handsome black bear. Every creature in the woods knew without a doubt that Brutus was in charge. He taught each of them the same thing. He'd say, "If you don't want rock salt in your backside, you had better learn to respect Farmer John's place."

Bear Facts

Zoologists recognize seven species of bears: big brown bears; American black bears; Asiatic black bears; polar bears; sun bears; sloth, or Indian bears; and spectacled bears. In addition, many zoologists classify the giant panda as a bear.

Bears are large, heavy, meat-eating mammals. They are found throughout all of the Northern Hemisphere and in some parts of the tropics, but not in Africa or Australia.

In their structure and teeth, bears are related most closely to the dog family. They have a large body and head with short, strong limbs and short tails. The jaws are extended and powerful, while the teeth are large and well adapted for crushing food. The eyes and ears are small, and their eyesight and hearing are not as good as their sense of smell. The limbs have long and powerful claws that are used for tearing and digging, as well as for fighting and killing animals for food. The whole sole of the bear's foot rests upon the ground, and the bear leaves a footprint resembling that of a man.

The bear's coat of fur is long and shaggy and usually is a shade of brown, black, or white.

Bears are rather slow and clumsy when they move; yet almost all bears, except the heaviest, climb trees, and all are agile in climbing over rocks and ice. When enraged or frightened, they can cover ground at great speed. Most bears are wanderers and, in tropical and temperate regions, are active in the evening and at night.

Bears are omnivorous and feed on plants, insects, fish, and some larger animals. Some may raid herds of swine and cattle and flocks of sheep. Some bears, such as the Alaskan brown bear, or Kodiak, live almost entirely on fish. Bears also eat ants, honey-making bees, and wasps. They dip up anthills and overturn rotting logs and stumps to find ants, and they search out bee honeycombs and tear them to pieces for the honey. They also eat juicy leaves and herbs, roots, fruit, sweet acorns, and berries.

Bears generally live alone except during the mating and breeding season. They live in caves, crevices among the rocks, hollow logs, or dense thickets. One kind is aquatic. During the winter, bears stay in a deep winter sleep, which is similar to hibernation except that their body temperature is not reduced and their bodily functions continue.

One litter of one to four young is born each year (usually after hibernation) after a gestation period of six to nine months. The young remain with the mother until they are fully grown. Their life span is fifteen to thirty years when wild; one animal in captivity reached an age of forty-seven years.

American black bears, like Brutus, are found in many large wooded areas of North America and south to Mexico. There are about seventy-five thousand of them in the national forests of the United States. Many states allow people to hunt these bears during certain seasons, and hunters kill about twenty-five thousand a year.

The black bear is usually black, although it may be brown, reddish, yellowish, or cream-colored.

They grow about five feet long and are the smallest bears of North America. Most black bears are from two hundred to three hundred pounds, but some weigh up to five hundred pounds.

Black bears can run as fast as twenty-five miles per hour when they chase prey, and they are skillful tree climbers. These bears become troublesome around camps and cabins if food is left in their reach. Black bears have severely injured, and sometimes have even killed, campers or travelers who feed them.

Black bears climb easily and wander extensively. They feed on both animal and plant life, and occasionally they raid livestock. They are timid and secretive and rarely are dangerous unless wounded or cornered. They often are captured and tamed.